Napoleon

Written by Kim Kennedy
Illustrated by Kim Kennedy and Doug Kennedy

VIKING

Napoleon is a crafty little dog.

When it rains, and he can't go outside to play,

he goes up to the attic.

If he's lucky, the roof will leak.

He likes to catch the drops in tin cups.

Then, while the drops land *plinkety-plink*,

he digs through his treasure box.

Sometimes he finds a hat.

Or a cowboy boot,

which makes him want to . . .

. . . rob a train.

When it thunders,

and his shadow starts to shake,

Napoleon conducts experiments with bubbles...

. . . and lightning.

He rests for a while and reads old newspapers.

He thinks about things as he flips the crunchy pages.

Then he drags a dusty coat across the floor . . .

... and hangs Christmas decorations on it.

After all that work,

Napoleon stands back and admires his beautiful mess.

Finally, he crawls into bed for a nap,
and drifts off to the sound of his cups ringing
plinkety-plink, plinkety-plink.

For
our family
and
William Joyce

VIKING
Published by the Penguin Group
Penguin Books USA Inc., 375 Hudson Street, New York, New York 10014, U.S.A.
Penguin Books Ltd, 27 Wrights Lane, London W8 5TZ, England
Penguin Books Australia Ltd, Ringwood, Victoria, Australia
Penguin Books Canada Ltd, 10 Alcorn Avenue, Toronto, Ontario, Canada M4V 3B2
Penguin Books (N.Z.) Ltd, 182–190 Wairau Road, Auckland 10, New Zealand

Penguin Books Ltd, Registered Offices: Harmondsworth, Middlesex, England

First published in 1995 by Viking, a division of Penguin Books USA Inc.

1   3   5   7   9   10   8   6   4   2

Text copyright © Kimberly Kennedy, 1995
Illustrations copyright © Kimberly Kennedy and Doug Kennedy, 1995
All rights reserved

LIBRARY OF CONGRESS CATALOGING-IN-PUBLICATION DATA
Kennedy, Kim.
Napoleon / written by Kim Kennedy;
illustrated by Kim Kennedy and Doug Kennedy.   p.   cm.
Summary: Napoleon the dog amuses himself on a rainy day by spending
time in the attic catching raindrops in tin cups, rummaging through his treasure box,
reading old newspapers, and decorating an old coat with Christmas ornaments.
ISBN 0-670-86404-8 (hardcover)
[1. Dogs—Fiction. 2. Play—Fiction.] I. Kennedy, Kim, ill. II. Title.
PZ7.K3843Nap 1995 [E]—dc20 95-4578 CIP AC

Printed in China
Set in Deligne